Lucky Leaf

KEVIN O'MALLEY

WALKER & COMPANY

NEW YORK

First published in the United States of America in 2004 by Walker Publishing Company, Inc.

Published simultaneously in Canada by Fitzhenry and Whiteside, Markham, Ontario L3R 4T8

For information about permission to reproduce selections from this book,
write to Permissions, Walker & Company, 104 Fifth Avenue, New York, New York 10011

Library of Congress Cataloging-in-Publication Data

O'Malley, Kevin, 1961–
Lucky Leaf / Kevin O'Malley.
p. cm.
Summary: After his mother tells him to stop playing video games and go outside,
a young boy tries to catch the last leaf on a tree, thinking it will bring him luck.
ISBN 0-8027-8924-2(HC) — ISBN 0-8027-8925-0 (RE)
[1. Luck—Fiction. 2. Leaves—Fiction. 3. Video games—Fiction.] I. Title

PZ7.O526Lu 2004
[E]—dc22
2003068868

The illustrations for this book were inked on layout paper with a Hunt nib and colored in PhotoShop.

Book design by Nicole Gastonguay

Visit Walker & Company's Web site at
www.walkeryoungreaders.com

PRINTED IN HONG KONG

2 4 6 8 10 9 7 5 3

FOR NOAH AND CONNOR —K. O